Wizard of Oz

Illustrated by Eric Kincaid

Dorothy lived with her Aunt Em and Uncle Henry. She had a small dog called Toto.

One day there was a whirlwind. Dorothy and Toto were alone in the house. The whirlwind lifted them up high into the sky.

The house came to rest in the Land of the Munchkins. It fell on top of the Wicked Witch of the East and killed her.
The Munchkins were very pleased. They gave Dorothy the Wicked Witch of the East's magic shoes.

"Can you help me find my way home?" she asked the Munchkins. They shook their heads. They did not know the way.

"Go to the Emerald City," they said. "Ask the Wizard of Oz to help you."

Dorothy put on the magic shoes and set off along the yellow brick road with Toto.

After many miles Dorothy met a Scarecrow. "Can I go to the Emerald City with you?" said the Scarecrow. "Perhaps the Wizard of Oz will give me a brain."

The next day they found a Tin Man in the forest. "Can I go with you?" said the Tin Man. "Perhaps the Wizard of Oz will give me a heart."

A Lion jumped out of the bushes and roared. It tried to bite Toto. Dorothy slapped the Lion.

"How dare you bite a little dog! You are a coward!" said Dorothy.

"I know," said the Lion. "But how can I help it? Do you think the Wizard of Oz would give me some courage?"

They went across ditches and over rivers. At last they came to the Land of Oz. They went to the Emerald City. Everything in the city was green.

The Wizard of Oz lived in a palace. He was a magician. He could change the way he looked.

In the Throne Room all Dorothy could see was a huge green head. "I am Oz," said a voice. "Who are you and why do you seek me?" Dorothy told him she wanted to find the way home. "I will help if you kill the Wicked Witch of the West," said the Wizard.

The Scarecrow saw the Wizard as a green lady.

The Tin Man saw the Wizard as a wild animal.

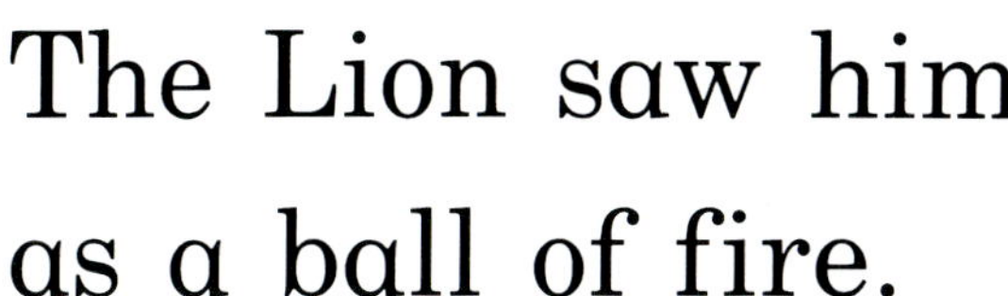

The Lion saw him as a ball of fire.

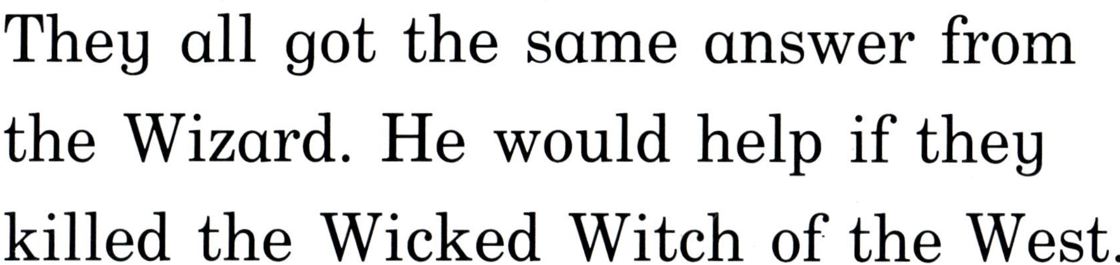

They all got the same answer from the Wizard. He would help if they killed the Wicked Witch of the West.

The Wicked Witch of the West saw them coming. She tried to stop them.

The Tin Man killed the wolves. The Scarecrow caught the crows. The bees broke their stings when they tried to sting the Tin Man. The Winkies ran away when the Lion roared.

The Wicked Witch of the West was angry. She sent the fierce Flying Monkeys after them. They dropped the Tin Man on to some rocks. He broke into pieces. They pulled the straw out of the Scarecrow. They put the Lion into a cage.

The Flying Monkeys took Dorothy and Toto to the Wicked Witch's castle. The Witch saw Dorothy's magic shoes and began to shake. The Wicked Witch kicked Toto. That made Dorothy very angry.

She picked up a bucket of water and threw it over the Witch. Then as Dorothy looked on in wonder, the Witch began to shrink and fall away. Then there was nothing but a puddle. The Wicked Witch of the West was dead.

Dorothy let the Lion out of the cage. The Winkies helped her put the straw back into the Scarecrow. They helped her put the Tin Man back together.

When they returned to the palace the Throne Room was empty. The Lion gave a roar and knocked over a screen. Hiding behind it was a little man. It was the Wizard. "I am not really a wizard," he said. "People only think I am because I can do tricks. But I will help you if I can."

The Wizard filled the Scarecrow's head with sharp things like pins and needles. "Now you have a brain," he said.

He took a red silk heart stuffed with sawdust and put it inside the Tin Man.

He gave the Lion a drink that would give him courage.

He made a balloon so that Dorothy and Toto could fly home. The balloon took off before Dorothy was ready. It flew away without her.

The Good Witch of the South came to rescue Dorothy.

"Tap your heels together three times and tell the magic shoes where you want to go," she said.

The Good Witch of the South made the Scarecrow ruler of the Emerald City. She made the Tin Man ruler of the Winkies. She made the Lion King of the Forest.

Dorothy and Toto went home to Aunt Em and Uncle Henry.

All these appear in the pages of the story. Can you find them?

Dorothy and Toto

Scarecrow

Tin Man

Wicked Witch